MW01094639

LAST
FLIGHT
OF THE
GODDESS

KEN SCHOLES

LAST
FLIGHT
OF THE
GODDESS

KEN SCHOLES

FAIRWOOD PRESS
Auburn • Seattle

LAST FLIGHT OF THE GODDESS
A Fairwood Press Book
November 2006
Copyright © 2006 by Ken Scholes

Fairwood Press
5203 Quincy Ave SE
Auburn, WA   98092
www.fairwoodpress.com

Cover, Jacket & Book Design
by Patrick Swenson

ISBN: 0-9789078-0-9
ISBN13: 978-0-9789078-0-8
First Fairwood Press Edition: November 2006
Printed in the United States of America

For Jen,
the Fiercest and the Fairest of them All

INTRODUCTION
by Jay Lake

I first met Ken Scholes sometime in 2001. Norwescon, perhaps, or World Horror Con. He's a big man, bigger than me, and louder, with a more demonstrative sense of humor. Though I suppose the reality is more sordid and intermittent, in retrospect, it seems like we instantly bonded.

Around the same time I reviewed a little story called "Edward Bear and the Very Long Walk," which appeared in *Talebones* #22, in the spring of that year. It was, and is, a fabulous story, available these days in a reprint online at *Revolution SF*. Oddly enough, this gem of a story was by a guy named Ken Scholes.

Naturally I failed to put the two together.

Now it's five years later. Ken's grown a writing career for himself — winning L. Ron Hubbard's Writers of the Future Contest, appearances in all kinds of markets from *Talebones* (again and again) to *Realms of Fantasy*, as well as in several markets I've edited or co-edited — *44 Clowns, TEL : Stories* and *Polyphony 6*. And what he's grown into is one of those twisty, gifted, unclassifiable writers. The kind our genre loves to love and never knows quite what to do with.

And here Fairwood Press has gone and put *Last Flight of the Goddess* into a book of his own. There'll be no living with the boy now.

There's a bunch of things you might not know about Ken. He can simultaneously do impressions of Bob Dylan and the Queen of England. His orange bicycle tale is by far the most wretchedly funny bar story I've ever heard, all the more so for being utterly auto-biographical. His childhood is even stranger than mine, and that's going some. He's a former boy preacher, teenage prodigy who had a Baptist congregation for a while, before lapsing into the gentle, compassionate humanism I've come to know him for. He's married to the beautiful and talented Jen West. And as he'll tell you, Ken is the world's only metrosexual redneck.

Take all those bits and pieces of a man's life, mix them with the quirky science fantasy and magical realism he's been banging out over the years, and you've got *Last Flight of the Goddess*. First and foremost it's a love letter. But since Ken's one of *us*, the love letter is addressed to his wife, to Robert E. Howard and Gary Gygax, and to the whole tradition of our field.

So follow him through this flight, and see what the bubbling ferment that is Ken Scholes can do for you. He's a genius in the process of happening. Here's your chance to get in early.

Portland, Oregon
September, 2006

LAST
FLIGHT
OF THE
GODDESS

*J*shed no tears when I put the torch to my wife. I suppose I could have. Who would fault an old man his grief?

That morning, as Bambilo Broadback helped me strap on my breastplate, fasten my greaves, and put on my gauntlets, I thought about the crowd I expected. Old faces and nearly forgotten names representing a time that had moved on when I was a younger man. While he huffed and puffed to make those recently polished relics fit, I wondered who would attend. Surely the Crown Prince and his consort upon shiny white stallions and beneath purple and gold banners. And Azerminus the Mage, of course. And Fenruk Ironmauler and the three pretty, young prostitutes he passed off as his wives. The list marched on and on. We'd sent messenger birds everywhere.

But when the moment came it was a small gathering. Henry the Livery Man. Jacko and some of the old regulars from the tavern stood there in their Restday Best. Margi Fenroper and some of my dearly departed's other friends. And a priest older than I that stank of last night's beer. He said a few words. I said a few words. No one else spoke.

We'd dressed her in her finest silk robes. Bambilo's wife, Buckabith, had painted my wife's face and fancied up her hair.

In life, as the years crept on, we'd talked about death. I'd always said "Roll me to yonder creek; feed those damnable trout that have vexed me so long." No hero's send-off for me, though years back I bore the title. And she had always said "Give me back to the sky." In my mind, I'd envisioned my Luendyl on a pyre shining in her armor with Shymalius's twin scimitars clenched in her white fists and the Demigoddess Gladenda's Helm of Knowing masking her face. But retirement brings new priorities, and gradually all our glammered accouterments bought us a hearth, a home, a quiet place to raise our daughter. In my mind, I'd also envisioned a throng of grief-struck nobles, heroes, fans, and hopefuls.

In the end, a near dozen of us gathered around a pile of alder logs, and I set torch to the most beautiful woman I had ever seen.

*S*he fell from the sky like a goddess. I remember it well. I was camped in the heart of the Blastlands, the ruins of Ghul-Shar-Tov on the horizon painted silver by the rising moon. I heard a rustling in the air, followed by muttered curses, and then a yelp as she spun down and thudded into my tent, knocking it down and tangling herself in the canvas.

"Damn," the goddess said. "Damned damnable damnation."

She was beautiful. My first impulse was to laugh, but when the moonlight caught her long red hair, her face, her sleek form, her armor-entrusted breasts, my humor failed. And my words as well.

She stomped her feet, and I realized they were sparking and smoking. A pair of highly unreliable Oingeltonken's Flights of Fancy Winged Shoes fluttered and flapped their last. Finally, she looked up.

"What are you staring at, soldier?" Her hand moved towards the hilt of a scimitar at her waist. I remember thinking at the time that it looked a bit like one of Shymalius's fabled twin blades, but then her breasts distracted me again.

I shook my head. "Nothing," I said and thought better of it. "Everything."

She smiled. That's really all there was to it. It hooked me in a way my lures and worms could never hook the leaping trout of Brookwood Down.

Her eyes narrowed and shifted towards the ruined city behind me. "Here for the treasure then?"

"No. Renown. Prestige. You know."

"Nobility," she said. "How nice."

"And you?"

She sized me up. I was a pup then. I'd just slain my first giant the winter before. More an accident really — he'd fallen onto my lance and I'd then put my long sword in his ear. Still, it had netted me a reputation. I was wearing my lower-end Yorlund's Eye-Blinding Plate Mail Extravaganza. I filled it out nicely and had all my hair in those days. She must have felt whatever I felt, too, because her smile stretched across her face like a cool river. "I'll take whatever I can get," she said.

It started fast between us and lasted most of the night. In the morning, after we'd sorted out whose armor and undergarments were whose, we routed the beasts from Ghul-Shar-Tov and pillaged a small fortune from its catacombs and vaults.

It started fast between us. And lasted the rest of my life.

*T*he tears came that night in the tavern. Slow at first, then an unstoppable rush. Only a few were there to see it.

"Andro?"

I looked up through water. "Yes, Bambilo?"

"It's okay to cry."

Halflets and Fey make lots of talk about being in touch with the child inside, about expressing your feelings and all that *Venison Stew for the Heart* crap. I subscribed more to Berserker Bronbur's time-tested wisdom: "When angry, smash stuff. When sad, smash more stuff." But the image of her pyre took the fight out of me. I pushed aside my empty beer mugs, hid my face in my hands, and just let loose with it.

Ten minutes or so passed. Bambilo patted my shoulder. "She was a good woman."

I snuffled. "The best."

"She was a strong woman."

"The strongest." I sniffed and wiped my nose on the sleeve of my tunic. I felt composure leaking back into me.

Bambilo sighed. "It's a shame Karysa couldn't be here for it."

And that started the tears all over again.

*A*t first, I thought I hadn't heard her correctly. We were back to back under the torture dome of the Demon King of Zharid Keep. Blood made the floor slippery, but his minion Gibbers rushed on and we piled up their bodies around us. I brought Fangblade down to spark and split a Gibber helmet, dodging to the right to avoid being skewered by a spear.

There was a brief lull, and I glanced over my shoulder at her. "What did you say?"

Luendyl had both scimitars by now. We'd been together for nearly ten years. We'd slain fierce foes, rescued fair damsels and girlish princes, won and lost two kingdoms and a dozen fortunes. Those blades whirled and spun, limbs flying and blood splashing. "I don't want to do this anymore," she said again. "It's not good for the baby."

I took off a Gibber arm. "The what?"

Two more fell behind me, gurgling and kicking. "The baby, Andro. Our baby."

My sword arm came down and I turned to face her. "I thought you were using Azerminus's Egg Charming Elixir?"

She sliced through a Gibber as it lunged at me. "I was."

Another darted in, its eyes wide and its mouth gaping. I paused to run it through and turned back to her. "Then *what* happened?"

She shrugged, then brought both blades down on the Gibber Chieftain's skull-helmet. "Remember those damned winged shoes I was wearing when we met?"

I looked around. We were the only two left standing. "Yes?"

She smiled that smile that had hooked me a decade ago. "Magic can be a fickle thing."

I remember a hundred thoughts rushing me at once. Andro Giantslayer . . . a father. The deposed King Andro of Grunland . . . a father. A father. A father. A father. My heart caved in, then expanded. I sheathed Fangblade, that glimmering sword carved and enchanted from a dragon's tooth.

She sheathed her blades. Her blue eyes searched mine and began to twinkle. "Well?"

"Well." I scratched my head. "I suppose we could sell off some of our gear and buy that place near Brookwood you liked so well."

She threw herself at me. I can still hear the crash of metal today. I can still taste her mouth on mine.

After the kiss, she pulled back and drew her blades again. "Sell our stuff? Are you mad?" She pointed to the door to the Demon King's throne room. "Let's finish what we've started and buy the whole damned town."

"And the river," I said thinking about the fish I'd seen jumping there last spring. "I'm going to need a new hobby."

For the next two hours we savored every moment of our last fight together. Of course, we had no way of knowing then that the Demon King had bankrupted his treasury the winter before.

I drank too much that night after the funeral but Jacko did not cut me off. He kept the mugs coming. He'd lost his wife the year before.

When it was down to just the two of us, I lunged to my feet.

"I've a cot in the back," Jacko said.

"I've a bed at home," I said. The room wobbled. Or perhaps it was me.

"Tomorrow then."

"Goodnight, Jacko." I left the tavern. Outside, the village slept as dogs barked beneath a starry sky.

I took the forest path along the creek and listened to the water dance across the rocks. Evergreen and wood smoke scented the night air. I reached our dark little house in the clearing and paused at the door, my hand outstretched towards the latch.

Turning, I made my way around the house and up the hill behind it. The fire had burned itself out. I walked to the center of the charred wood and piles of ash and sat down.

"Luendyl," I said. "I don't know what to do."

The tears came back and at some point in the night, I stretched myself out over her, and fell asleep.

I dreamed about goddesses falling from the sky, and when the morning sun woke me up, I knew what to do.

I ran to the house, raced in and kicked aside my pile of armor from yesterday's service. I took down an urn from the mantle. It bore the crest of the Kings of Devyn, stamped into its platinum surface.

We'd never sold it, though we'd been tempted. We'd put aside plenty for our future, and when Karysa'd hit her stride, she'd started sending a bit home now and again. I took the urn outside to the creek and unscrewed its top.

"Sorry, Falgron," I said as I dumped its contents into the water. "You were a faithful steed to the last but I've no need for you any longer." I suppose I could have found another urn if I'd stopped to think about it. But I didn't.

I went back to the top of the hill. I scooped handfuls of my wife mingled with alder ash until the urn was full. I replaced the cap.

"Are you ready, Luendyl?"

Back inside, I set her next to my armor. Henry had used old bridle scraps to lengthen the straps. My broad shoulders and heavy chest had dropped closer to the middle now. My hands and joints ached from a hundred battles. Still, I managed to suit myself up without

Bambilo's help. I pulled a tarnished sword down from the wall and buckled its belt around my waist. Nothing like Fangblade, but what blade ever was? Next, I packed my rucksack, nestling the urn down amid clean socks, a blanket, some rolled up clothes, a crust of bread, and a bit of cheese.

When I turned to the door, a boy stood there waiting.

He was maybe fourteen. Soft-faced and big-eyed, hair poking out from beneath a green cap. He had a lute slung over his shoulder.

We stared at each other and finally the boy spoke. "Are you Andro Giantslayer?" He was trying too hard to deepen his voice. That should have been my first clue.

"Yes." The weight of my armor, sword, and pack toppled me. I dropped to the floor and hoped it looked like I was just sitting down quickly.

"Exiled King of Grunland?"

I shrugged out of the pack. "Yes."

"The Finisher of Fang the Dread?"

"Yes."

"Founder of the Heroes League of Handen Hall?"

"Yes." I paused. "I had help."

"Father of Karysa the White of the West?"

I felt pride bloom. "Yes."

"Husband of Luendyl the Fierce?"

I swallowed. "And Fair."

"Huh?"

"Luendyl the Fierce and Fair," I said. "Yes."

"Is this a bad time?"

I looked at my pack, at my armored legs stretched out on the floor, the sword sheath pinned beneath them in an uncomfortable way. "The worst possible," I said. "What do you want?"

The boy blushed. That should have been my second clue. "I've come a long way. From Alderland through Mistvale along the Dragon's Spine Mountains."

"You're vexing me."

"Last month, the Emperor of Shaluzan announced a contest among minstrels. He swore by the jade throne that the musician with the most moving song would be granted title, land and —" The boy moved his hands in a wide, exaggerated arch. "—And vast wealth beyond anyone's wildest imaginings."

The way he moved his hands, the way he moved his hips. My third clue. I opened my mouth. Closed it. Thought a minute. Looked closer at his face and eyes. "Aren't you really a girl?"

"No."

"I think you are."

"I most certainly am not."

I shrugged, then climbed to my feet, leaving the pack on the floor. "Makes no never mind to me," I said. "Boy or girl, help a tired old man with his pack and I'll help you with your song."

"It has to be original," the girl said as she picked up my luggage. "And very moving."

"I'll see what I can do."

We walked out the door and into the summer sun. "And pretty, too," she said.

I looked down at her. I could see my daughter in her face now. The short, crazy hair underneath the cap. The awkward walk with my pack slung over her shoulder. I couldn't think of anything else to say so I repeated myself. "I'll see what I can do."

*W*e were fishing, my daughter and I, up-creek behind the house. I remember it was summer then, too. I held my rod — an enchanted bit of bamboo that Azerminus had brought on his last visit — and watched the ripples in the deep parts of the water. Karysa poked at a rotten stump with a stick.

"I've been thinking," she said. She was fourteen I think.

"Yes?" I shifted my weight on the boulder. Even back then, my joints got stiff.

Her stick followed a beetle's scurrying trail. "I don't want to marry Bambilo's son after all."

Bambilo Broadback had settled in on the farm just the other side of town. He and Buckabith had a litter of Halflet kids and the oldest, Bondilo, had made our daughter his solemn quest to win. I'd never taken it seriously.

"Really?"

Karysa nodded. "First of all, I don't really like boys very much."

I grunted. "Because you're too busy trying to be one."

She ignored me. "No, I know what I want to do when I grow up."

"What's that?"

"I want to be a hero. Like you."

Since that day in Zharid Keep, I'd done the odd job here and there. To keep my skills and blade sharp, I always told my Luendyl. Karysa had grown up with it. "And your mother, too," I said. "She was quite the hero in her day."

"Was," Karysa said. "But she quit."

"Sure. To have *you*." I reached over with my free hand and mussed her hair. "Trust me. No gibber, dragon, troll, or giant ever gave your mother half the fuss you have."

She laughed. I laughed too. I held my rod out to her. "Want to give it a try?"

She took it from me and stood up, her face serious as she watched the water. "I'll bet I'll be a great hero. The greatest. Why —"

But at that moment, a trout hit the line hard, and as she pulled it in, I knew she was right.

Someday my daughter's heroics would be legendary. Of this I had no doubt.

The minstrel girl and I walked all day. As the sun set over forested hills, we pulled aside of the King's Way and made camp. She'd carried her pack, my pack, and the lute all day and hadn't slowed down once. I had gasped and coughed and wheezed my way beside her.

"Should I build a fire?"

I nodded, winded.

"And then we can work on my song?"

I nodded again and waved her away.

Later, with the fire roaring, I shared my bread and cheese with her. "We'll hit town tomorrow and stock up," I said. After we'd eaten, she picked up her lute and tuned it.

"So where are you going?" she asked, her fingers moving across frets and adjusting knobs.

"I'm taking my wife out for one last adventure."

She wrinkled her nose. "I don't think we've known each other long enough for me to be considered your wife. Besides, you're too old."

"I thought you said you were a boy?"

"Oh yeah. I did, didn't I?"

I chuckled. "There's nothing wrong with being a

girl. Gods know I've told my daughter the same thing a hundred, hundred times." I reached for the rucksack and drug out the urn. "Anyway, I didn't mean you. I meant my wife." I tapped the lid.

"You mean Luendyl the Fierce?"

"And Fair," I said. "Yes."

She gulped. "In there?"

"Yes. She passed three nights ago." I felt the tears coming but this time held them back. I could feel my lower lip quiver.

"You must be very sad."

I nodded. "More so than you could imagine."

"I can imagine," she said. "I'm alone, too, now. My folks passed about five years back. Troll raids in this little border town where we lived." She picked out a melody, frowned and twisted the knobs a bit more.

"I'm sorry to hear it." I threw another stick into the fire. The sound of the lute could not cover our silence. "Well, enough about loss," I finally said. "Sing me a song about life."

"And after, you'll tell me stories?"

"Yes. We'll start on that song of yours. Win you your title and land."

"And wealth," she said.

"Of course."

She closed her eyes and drew in a breath. The melody from her fingers grew louder; her voice lilted up and out, strong and sweet and clear as a brook. I'd never heard that tune before. Or if I had, I'd never heard it sung so well.

*A*fter the song, after the stories, I dreamed of Luendyl. She sat across from me by the fire and watched the girl sleep.

"She reminds me of Karysa," I said.

Luendyl smiled. It was a playful smile with a bit of sadness about the edges. "What are you doing, old man?"

"I'm taking you on one last adventure."

"You're crazy. You're too old to be out jollivating around in that get-up." In my dreams, I'm always wearing my armor and sword.

"You told me to give you back to the sky."

"And how do you suppose you'll do that?"

I shrugged. "I'll figure it out."

"One suggestion?"

"Yes?"

Her grin showed teeth this time. "Whatever you do, don't use Oingeltonkel's flying shoes."

I laughed. "No. I don't suppose I will."

Luendyl looked at the sleeping girl. "Andro?"

"Yes, my love?"

"It's been a whole day and you still don't know her name. You really should ask."

"Not sure she'll tell me. She thinks she's a boy."

Luendyl laughed. The music of it was quite like the song earlier. "Sounds familiar, doesn't it?"

It did.

A boot in my side brought me awake. Time was, not even a haunt could sneak up on me. Not so now. I jumped and sat up.

"What have we here? An old man and his grand-daughter off to the fair?" A group of five men stood in the midst of our camp. They wore dark forest-colored clothes, bows slung over shoulders, and knives glinting in their hands. A pre-dawn gray wrapped the woods around us, and the road shimmered like white water.

"Perhaps," another one said, "'Tis no grandfather at all but a buggerly girl-grabber. What say you, girl?"

The girl sat up. She looked angry. "I'm not a girl. I'm not a girl at all."

"That doesn't make it any better," I told her. "Keep quiet and I'll handle this." I struggled to stand. Another boot tipped me over.

"Stay down, old man." This one was the leader. I could always just tell by the look of one. "If you coop-erate, we'll leave you to your lechery. And if not —" he pointed his knife at me and etched a cross in the air. "No more girls for you."

Three days of grief washed out in anger. I can't remember how long it had been since I'd felt a rage coming on. Years perhaps. Dozens of years more likely. I bottled it as fast as it built, stored it up, and felt around under my blanket for the hilt of my sword. "It's my coin you'll be wanting, I suspect."

The bandit leader laughed. "That too." He backed away, eyes never leaving me, and scooped up the urn. "Platinum, boys. Pure platinum like I said."

Purple spots crowded my vision. I tightened my grip on the sword. I'd learned years ago to never sleep with it in plain view or sheathed, a habit that had saved me more than once. I felt my muscles tighten, and the world slowed down around me.

"Let." My hand moved like water, sliding the sword out from under the blanket. "Go." My other hand flattened itself against the ground. "Of." My legs coiled and creaked beneath me as I pushed myself up. "My." The sword came up as the bandit, too late, tried to leap backwards. "Wife."

I could have taken his head off. Or at least partially. But at the last minute, I turned the blade and smacked him in the temple with the flat of my sword. He went over fast, dropping my wife as he fell.

The girl scrambled from her blankets to grab up his knife while I stood over him with the point of my sword at his throat.

He recovered quickly. "There are five of us and

two of them," he said. "Don't just stand there . . . get them."

His four companions exchanged glances. Their faces were white in the morning gloom. They didn't look like they were in a hurry at all.

I grinned down at him. "I think your friends might be smarter than you." My anger burned out fast, replaced with surprise at how easy it came back. I hadn't moved like that in years. It felt good. I'd pay for it later, of course. "And if they're as smart as I think they are, they'll be leaving soon."

They turned and bolted. Most bandits are a cowardly lot.

"As to you," I said. "I'll be having *your* coin now."

He slowly untied the small purse at his belt and set it on the ground.

"And now, an apology for the girl and me."

"I'm not a —"

I turned my head and let her see my scowl. She closed her mouth.

"Apologies, Sir and Lady." The girl kicked the fire a bit, eyes flashing mad.

"Now off with you." He scuttled away from me like a crab, then stood and turned in the direction his friends had gone. "No, no," I said. "Not *that* way. The other way. You can find your friends later. After we've gone."

Something like gratitude mixed with a sneer twisted his face. He opened his mouth to speak, thought better of it, and ran away.

The girl stared at me. "That's going in the song," she said. "Definitely."

"You haven't seen anything yet," I told her. "By the way?"

"Yes?"

"My wife told me I should ask you your name."

She looked at the urn. Then she looked back at me. "No she didn't."

"Yes. She did. Last night."

"I think I'll leave that bit out of the song."

"Whatever you say. It's your song."

She started rolling her blanket, gathering her things, shoving them into her pack. I sat down, suddenly a bit shaken.

"Andrillia," she finally said. "My name is Andrillia."

"So you *are* a girl?"

She glowered at me. "Don't push it."

*T*ime was, every village boasted two or three Andros or Andrillias. I think the first Andro I met was a boy of maybe four years. A pretty woman opened the door of her hovel and shouted as I was passing through her small town. Falgron was in his prime back then, massive and white, hooves striking sparks on the cobblestones.

"Andro, come in for supper!"

I reined in and dismounted. "That's very kind of you, Madam."

She looked frightened. A large armored man and a large armored horse towering over her on her porch. She started to speak when a small voice rang out up the street.

"Coming, Mom." A boy lightning-flashed by me and into the house.

By then, Luendyl caught up with me. "Are we stopping?"

"That boy has my name," I said, nodding to the house.

Luendyl smiled. "Sometimes you're quite oblivious. Do you know that?"

I frowned. "What?"

"We've passed through hundreds of towns and villages. There have been Andros and Andrillias in every one of them since that little bit with Charnak the Terrible and the Six Princesses of Arghulistan. I think it tipped the scales a bit on that prestige of yours."

"Oh. That." I smiled at the memory of it. "I had help." I looked at my wife, sitting high and proud and beautiful in the saddle. "And I haven't seen any little Lues and Luendyls scampering about."

She smiled and nudged her horse forward. "That's because I'm one of a kind."

And always will be. I knew it then. I know it now.

*W*e bought a pony in the next town and tied our packs onto him. We also bought dried meat, more cheese and bread, and a few wineskins. When the storekeeper realized who I was, he threw in some spare socks and a wool cap for beneath my helmet. He warned me to keep my feet dry and my head covered. Andrillia had a purse of her own and bought more paper and ink.

We set out again that afternoon. The summer day held clear and warm. I thought about leaving off the armor but couldn't bring myself to do it. It rubbed my skin in places, it rode snug in others, and its weight pulled at me while the sun slowly cooked me. I left it on. Such journeys should not be comfortable.

"Where are we going?" Andrillia asked.

"North and then east," I said. "How did you get your name?"

"I think you saved my grandmother's life or something. I'm not sure."

"Probably did. I used to do that sort of thing a lot."

"I know. That's why I came looking for you. Only I didn't think you'd be so old."

I laughed. "I suppose I *am* old."

"You are," she said in a matter-of-fact way. "But that's okay. It'll make for a great song. Even if you die on the way."

"Thanks," I said.

"Don't mention it. Tell me about your daughter."

"She reminds me a lot of you," I told her. "But you like boys, right, even though you want to be one?"

I looked over at her. Andrillia frowned and thought about it. "Yeah. But don't tell anyone."

I nodded. We kept walking, and as we walked, I told her about Karysa.

I couldn't eat roast duck without thinking about her. Because when she showed up in our lives, the midwife who delivered Karysa stank of the roast duck she'd prepared for Restday dinner. And frankly, she was about the size of a roast duck when she came out.

She grew up too fast. We fought too much. We laughed a lot. We played a lot. We cried some. At fifteen, she learned the longsword. At sixteen, she learned the bow. The next year, we sold a few gems I'd plundered raiding a troglodyte lair and bought her that first suit of armor. Karysa had wanted to come with me but I'd refused.

"It's too dangerous. You could get hurt."

"So what?" she asked. "I'm not afraid of a couple of trogs." We were in the yard; she was practicing her dodge, thrust, and parry.

"A couple? Two dozen or more, most likely." I'd worked up a sweat as her sparring partner. She was good. "Out of the question."

I pressed her. She pressed back. Our swords clanked and clashed together.

Then I said it. Shouldn't have, but I did. "Maybe you should re-think this whole thing."

"What whole thing?" She still hadn't broken sweat. She had her father's height and her mother's looks. Of course, none of us knew where the white hair came from.

"The hero thing. It's really not that great."

"That's not how *you've* told it."

"Well, I was wrong. Besides, what about Bondilo Broadback?" Another dodge, thrust, and parry. "You could settle down. Get married. Have children." Our swords started to spark as she put more muscle into it. "It's quite rewarding."

She frowned at me. "Dad, I don't like boys."

I stopped, dropped my guard. "Don't like boys?"

"No. Never have."

"What's *that* supposed to mean?"

She stopped too. She shrugged. "I like girls. Just like you."

I didn't know what else to say so I said the obvious. "I only like your mother."

She sheathed her sword. "That's not what I mean."

"Oh." I just stood there and let it settle in. "Well, okay then," I finally said, "Bondilo has a sister, you know."

"Oh, Dad," she said and walked away.

A few minutes later, Luendyl came outside to see why I kept plunging my head into the trough and shouting curses at the horses. Her look alone was all the question she need ask.

"Our daughter likes girls," I said.

She cocked her head to the right and raised one eyebrow. "And?"

"That's all. She likes girls. Not boys."

Luendyl sighed. "Sometimes," she said slowly, "You are quite oblivious. Do you know that?"

I nodded. "I guess I am, aren't I? You've known for years, haven't you?"

She hugged me. My dripping head made her chest wet. "It's not the end of the world."

I stared at her breasts. I did that a lot, I guess. Armor, wet dresses, bare — it didn't matter; they fascinated me. "You're right. It's not. It's just not what I expected."

"Often the things we love best are what we expect least," she said. She saw where I was staring. "Remember that night in the Blastlands?"

"How could I ever forget?" I grinned, she caught my grin, and tossed it back. "Want to go inside or just do it right here?"

"Both," she said. And we did.

The next year, we bundled our little girl up in her very own suit of chain-mail and a shiny new sword and sent her off to make her mark upon the world.

We ran into a horde of gobbers on our third night under the stars. Actually, they ran into us. Gobbers are a bit shorter than gibbers but nearly as fierce and twice as stupid. Andrillia had just gone to fetch water when I heard the crash and crunch of many feet in the underbrush. I drew my sword.

They broke cover, shouting and shrieking, miscellaneous weapons gripped in their clawed hands. They poured past me as if I were a rock in the middle of their river. One of them took a half-hearted swing, putting a small dent into my side. I cut down a few, ran another through, and then they were gone. Behind them, I heard the baying of hounds and the crash of something even heavier moving towards us at breakneck speed.

Andrillia raced back into our small clearing. "What's going —"

A massive form hurtled towards us from the forest, interrupting her. It reared up, hooves flailing. Four large dogs blurred past, growling and howling, tearing up the ground in their pursuit of the gobbers. The dogs were my first clue. The smell of strong cologne, my second. I lowered my sword.

"Clovis?"

The hooves came down. "Aye. And who be you?"

"It's me. Andro."

Clovis sauntered forward. Centaurs as a whole made me uncomfortable. My head spun and my stomach lurched from their bizarre breeding tastes. Clovis was no exception. When Luendyl and I ran with him back in the day his eye went from human to horse to everything in between.

"Andro Giantslayer, by the Nine Hundred Toes of Erlik!" He towered over us, looking down, a bow and arrow held loosely in his right hand. "What in the Five Hells are you doing here?"

Andrillia spoke up. "He's out on one last adventure with his wife."

Clovis looked at the girl. He grinned. "A nice little filly. And where is Luendyl the Fair?"

"And Fierce," I said. "Luendyl the Fierce and Fair."

Somewhere over my shoulder, I heard gobbers screaming and dogs snarling. "It'll have to wait," Clovis said. "I've a-work to finish yonder." He reared again. The reek of perfumed oils filled the air. "But I'll be back shortly."

He slung his bow, drew two large axes, and galloped away.

Andrillia's face wrinkled and she held her nose. "He stinks."

I sheathed my sword and went back to building the fire. "You should smell him *without* the cologne," I said.

*W*hen Clovis returned, he hauled off the three gobbers I'd killed. "You're too old to be doing this," he said, slinging them over his back.

I didn't protest. The day's walk had worn me down.

Andrillia and I sat at the fire; Clovis stood at the edge of its light, shifting back and forth as the smoke changed course. He smacked his lips loudly. "And where's Luendyl?"

I nodded to the urn. I'd put her on the log beside me.

His face clouded. "She's gone then? Old friend, I'm sorry."

I felt loss in my throat again. It rose up from my stomach and closed off my words.

His large hand settled onto my shoulder. "She was a fine woman. A fierce warrior. A filly like no other."

I patted his hand. "She was indeed."

"And who is this? A granddaughter perhaps?"

Andrillia looked up from her script, her pen pausing between the paper and the ink bottle. "No. His daughter doesn't like boys."

Clovis arched his eyebrows. "Really?"

"Never mind, Clovis. She's a minstrel. She's tagging along collecting stories."

"Ah. Emperor Quon bin Jaheen and another of his damnable contests, I presume."

"And I mean to win it," Andrillia said. She went back to her writing. While she scribbled, Clovis and I passed a wineskin between us. His dogs hunkered down near the fire. Our pony worked at a bit of grass, a wide white eye turned in their direction.

"I'm truly sorry about Luendyl," Clovis said. "She was something to behold." He reached behind him, foraging in his saddlebags. "I have something that might help." He pulled out a tattered copy of *Venison Stew for the Heart* and offered it to me.

"Thanks, Clovis. It's not the help I'm needing, but thanks."

His eyes narrowed as he returned his book. "And what help *are* you needing?"

"The kind with wings."

Clovis chuckled. "Wings, eh? What are you up to, Andro?"

I shrugged. "A short flight. Over the Blastlands."

The centaur laughed. "They make those shoes, you know."

I shook my head. "I'm thinking something bigger. And more reliable."

He scratched his beard. Andrillia lifted her lute and began to pick out another melody. Clovis closed

his eyes. "I'd start with the King of Grunland," he finally said.

"He's not a big fan of mine."

"No, no . . . not the father. The son. The dad died
in a fishing accident years ago."

This piqued my interest. "I didn't know he fished."

"I think the fish had *him* actually. One of those
saber-toothed pikes the size of a wagon. Snarf." He
made a slurping noise and smacked his lips. "One bite
and that was that."

"And you don't think the son would have a grudge?"

"They got their bleeding throne back, didn't they?"
Clovis chuckled. "Besides, it was years ago. Years and
years."

"True enough."

"They'd be the closest, I'd wager. Though Azerminus
had a djinn at one point, I'd heard. That could work,
too."

"I wouldn't know where to find the codger."

Clovis snorted. "Surely he came for Luendyl's send-
off?"

"No. He didn't."

"Sent one of those singing scrolls?"

"No. He didn't."

I heard the growl and saw the eyes flash. "Why
that Gods-damned fop! I'd be ashamed to show my

head if I were him. What did the rest of the old gang have to say about that?"

I swallowed. "Nothing. The old gang didn't turn out."

Agitated, he pranced back from the fire, tore up some sod, and tossed his hair. "The old gang didn't turn out? For Luendyl the Fair's Farewell Pyre?"

"And Fierce," I said. "No. They didn't turn out."

I could tell he was working himself up to a lather over it. I couldn't think of anything else to say. "You know, Clovis?"

His voice bellowed out. "What?"

"You weren't there, either."

He stopped. He sauntered closer and yanked the wineskin from my hands, up-ending it into his mouth. Wine splashed down like red rain. "Bloody shame, that," he said. "Bloody shame."

*H*anden Hall at Godsfeast was a bright and merry place. We'd hired the few giants we hadn't killed to build it from old, old trees taken from the Elderwood. It was our last Godsfeast there, Luendyl and me. Her belly was swelling. She'd already sold off her armor and taken to silk robes. We'd just finished building our house on Brookwood Down.

Fenruk Ironmauler sat arm wrestling with Hamrung the Bold, an older hero of some renown who died not so long ago in the battle for Gremgol's Pass. Clovis the Hunter stood to the side, one arm draped around a mare and the other draped around a Bythulian dancing girl he'd recently rescued from some troll's stewpot. Dozens of others sat in various states of drunken recline. Azerminus the Mage brought the hall to order.

"Heroes League of Handen Hall," he said with a somber voice. "We come to the end of our feast and the end of an age."

"And the end of our ale," one of Dunder the Dwarflord's stepcousins added.

"Here, here," someone shouted.

"It gives me no pleasure to say it." Azerminus paused, then looked at Luendyl and me from beneath those jutting white eyebrows. "But Andro . . . Luendyl . . . you will be sorely missed."

"Here, here," a different voice said.

"Six years ago, we dozen heroes stood upon this ground, hallowed with the blood of our fallen, and covenanted together to build a hall to their memory that light would go out from this place into the lands." Azerminus was ever wordy and worse still when he had some wine in him. I can't remember the rest of what he said but there was much jest about the new adventure we stood on the edge of. At its conclusion, he gave Luendyl a satchel of magic diapers, and the roof rose with applause and laughter.

Luendyl gave him her sweetest smile. "They'd best work, Azerminus. For the years are creeping on you and you'll be a-needing some of these yourself before too long."

"And a pretty girl to put them on him," the stepcousin said in the midst of the uproar.

We stood at the front. We basked in the blessing of our friends. And after Clovis and his evening's work left giggling and pinching and neighing. And after Dunder gathered up his drunk friends to find a tavern. And after the hall lay quiet and stinking of alcohol, flatulence and cooked meat, the three of us sat down with a bottle Azerminus had managed to hide from the others. Luendyl waved off the wine in favor of some grazzelberry juice.

"I'll surely miss you," he said. He also cried easily and even more so with some wine in him. The tears coursed down his cheeks and into his beard, spattering his blue sequined robe. "I'll surely miss you both."

"But you'll come visit," Luendyl said.

"And go fishing," I added.

He nodded. "I will indeed. And I've heard of a magicker in Xantun who makes these amazing bamboo fishing poles."

Luendyl patted his hand. We drank some more.

"It won't be the same." He reached out a gnarled hand and patted Luendyl's stomach. "Still, what an adventure!"

We laughed. I caught her eye and saw the light dancing in it. I'd watched her decapitate hobgibbers in the White Wastes of Norlish. I'd seen her pluck the Crown Prince of Dervon from a giant's cooking pot. I'd raced with her through the skies beyond the Blastlands, arrows singing past us. But in all of the places, in all of the times, I had never seen her look happier than she was now. And I had never seen her look more beautiful.

"To parenting," Azerminus said and lifted his glass.

"To parenting," Luendyl and I said, and we all drank together.

The old wizard shook his head. "I still can't believe it."

Luendyl turned on that smile again. "Believe it, old man." She rubbed her belly. "I think that Egg Charming Elixir of yours needs a bit more work."

$\mathcal{W}$ e said our goodbyes to Clovis that morning. Under protest, I finally let him slip the copy of *Venison Stew* into my pack. I'd decided at the very least it could come in handy if kindling ran short. We entered Grunland six nights later without further misadventure.

But misadventure met us at the border.

"Names?" the fat guard asked.

"Andro Giantslayer," I said. I held up the urn. "And Luendyl the Fierce and Fair."

"And Andrillia," the girl added.

He scratched his beard and opened a scroll on his desk. He scratched some more, then stood. "Wait right here."

I was tired. That's my only excuse. We'd walked long hours that day. When he returned with a squad of Grunland Elite I didn't even reach for my sword.

"Andro the Usurper?" the Captain asked.

"Andro Giantslayer," I said.

"You are under arrest for high treason." He looked at Andrillia. "And your cohort as well. She looks a dangerous sort. There'll be no insurrection this day."

Then they took the urn, my sword, Andrillia's lute,

our bags, and Foster, our pony. They stripped off my armor and manacled my hands and feet. "This is ridiculous. I demand audience with Harvald at once."

The captain of the guard sneered. "What a coincidence. His Royal Highness demands audience with *you.*"

I was King of Grunland for exactly eight days, three hours and twenty-seven minutes the year after I met the love of my life and the year before I married her. I met Harvald the Second on my first day as king.

I remember the disapproving look Luendyl gave me as I dangled the wailing infant heir by his feet. She only needed to say one word. "Andro."

I looked at her. "Yes, my darling?"

"It's a baby. Not a toy."

I shrugged. "They shouldn't have left it lying about."

She took him from me. "You were chasing them with a sword."

Harvald the First had been tied up in the Gibber War of Aught Three. His queen, Drusilda, was frolicking with a dwarven acrobatics troupe at the summer palace in Rhendlis. I'd seen an opportunity and taken it. I didn't realize they'd left their son behind in the care of overly anxious nursemaids.

I shifted my crown. It made my head itchy. "Well, what do we do with it?"

She made little cooing noises at the baby. Little Harvald (a terrible name if you ask me) sputtered a bit more, and then gurgled a laugh. Babies are fickle things. "Is baby hungry or . . ." Luendyl sniffed at him. "Baby is *messy*."

I often repeat myself when I don't know what else to say. "What do we do with it?"

She scowled at me. "We change him, silly."

With the baby under one arm, she rummaged through a massive oak bureau etched with carvings of nymphs and fawns. She pulled out a diaper and knelt on the floor.

I've seen many sights. Severed limbs. Ditches of blood. The leftover gobbets of flesh in a dragon's bone pile. And I've smelled many smells. Charbroiled flesh. Week-old entrails. The toe-nail clippings of giants. Nothing I'd ever seen and nothing I'd ever smelled quite prepared me for this.

I fought back the nausea. "Gods, woman, what are you doing? Put that back on. Quickly."

She laughed. "Don't mind silly Andro. He just doesn't understand." After wadding up the messy cloth, she tickled the baby's stomach. "Don't mind him at all."

She was enjoying this too much. A dire thought slipped into my head. "You remembered your elixir today, right?"

She frowned at me. "Of course I did."

"Good."

She looked back at the baby. "But I'm going to want one of these someday."

My brain stumbled. It must've shown because she raised her eyebrows at me, waiting for my response. I ran five possible answers through my head before replying. "Uh . . . someday. Of course."

"Andro?"

"Yes dear?"

"I mean it. Someday." She fastened the clean diaper onto the little prince. "Hopefully, by then they'll have figured out diapers that change themselves."

"I'll speak to Azerminus," I said. "After all, I am a King now."

"You do that. How's the crown?"

"It itches," I said. "Don't know how much longer I can stand wearing the damnable thing."

I didn't need to worry about that, though. Eight days, three hours and six minutes later, Harvald the First brought his own and three neighboring armies to bear on my kingdom. And all for the sake of a baby who, frankly, seemed a lot happier when his parents were away. It would be a few more years before I understood that kind of love.

Parents are fickle things.

*M*y first words to Harvald the Second: "My, you've grown."

He was twice as fat as his father. I wasn't exactly sure how he fit his behind into the throne.

He leaned forward. The massive oak chair creaked. "Andro the Usurper," he said. "We are pleased to see you."

I looked around. Other than the guards and the girl, we were alone in the throne room. Light poured in through high stained-glass windows that depicted his father in a more robust and heroic manner than was necessarily true. "We are?" I asked.

He smiled. "Yes, we are."

"It's been a long time, Harvald. Last time I saw you, you had no teeth and soiled yourself regularly."

"And now *you* are the toothless pantaloons soiler." He laughed at his joke. Personally, I thought it was terrible humor.

I showed him my teeth. "No Diamblestori's Mystical Masticators here. As to the other — well, you'll just have to trust me. I may be old, but I'm not *that* old."

"And this is your army?" He looked at the girl. "We are amused."

I tried to move forward. The manacles clanked and the guards held me back. "Harvald, I am not seeking your throne. I retired years ago. I've actually come to ask for help."

This time, his laughter exploded from deep in his belly. Waves of fat shook and rolled. He continued laughing until big tears streamed down his cheeks.

I grinned as he composed himself. I thought maybe his humor was a good sign.

"What help would you ask of us?"

"Something with wings. For a short flight." I decided to appeal to his humanity. "My wife and I would be forever in your debt."

"And where *is* Luendyl the Usurpress?"

"Fierce and Fair," I said. "Luendyl the Fierce and Fair."

One of the guards stepped forward, holding the urn. "I think she's in here, your Highness."

His beady eyes narrowed. "Is she?"

I swallowed. I felt grief rustling in my belly. "She is."

For a moment I saw a spark, some kind of connection. Maybe some buried part of him remembered my wife's fond care. Or maybe we met on the even playing field of loss, his parents having both passed. Whatever it was, I decided to follow through.

I offered up my saddest smile. "Clovis the Hunter sent us. He thought you could help."

His eyes narrowed. "The centaur?"

"Yes."

The spark went out. His face went dark. He opened his mouth. "We'll not speak of him or the shame his cavorting caused my father." But then he did speak, the words tumbling over his fat lips. "To think of that beast and my mother rutting away in the stables. It broke my father's heart. He carried it with him to his deathbed."

I often say the wrong thing at the wrong time. "I thought your father died in a fishing accident?"

The gathering clouds on his face broke into a storm. "Enough." He muttered and blustered underneath his breath, shifting on his throne. He placed both his hands on his thighs and squeezed until his knuckles went white.

Andrillia stepped forward. "Your highness, may I speak?"

Harvald nodded.

She no longer looked like a girl pretending to be a boy. Instead, she was a young woman standing with confidence before the third most powerful man in the realm.

"Forgive my companion's insensitivity. Loss clouds his already questionable judgment." She bowed her head. "I beg your pardon on his behalf."

Harvald looked at her and then back at me. "Your daughter?"

I shook my head.

"Granddaughter?"

I shook it again. "A minstrel. She's gathering tales for her trade."

The storm passed. Interest replaced anger. "We would hear a tune, minstrel."

A guard pushed her lute into her hands. Andrillia offered a shy smile, swallowed, and began to play. The notes lifted into the high vaulted ceiling of the throne room, the stone walls throwing back the melody. When her voice joined the strings, it was like honeyed mead pouring over the tongue. She sang a song of famous deeds. The king nodded his approval. She sang a song of recent loss. The king wiped a tear. She sang a song of bawdy humor. The king slapped his knees and guffawed. And last, she sang their grand, sweeping national anthem "O Grunland Fair." It moved Harvald to his feet, his large body shaking.

Then Andrillia stopped, looked the king dead in his eyes, and bowed deeply.

"We are most pleased," Harvald said. He sat down.

"Thank you, your Highness." She handed the lute back to the guard and took her place beside me. "Will you help us?"

"They were good songs," he said. "It would be a shame to kill such talent." He turned to me. "Your companions have ever been your saving grace."

I had never heard truer words. I decided to keep quiet this time.

"Escort the lady minstrel to our guest quarters." Andrillia opened her mouth then closed it. She gave me a worried look but followed the guard out of the room. Harvald studied me as they left. "Our father had a dragon on contract."

"Of the winged variety?"

He nodded. "But she doesn't fly anymore. Not since her mate died. She doesn't do anything anymore. We send her cattle and gold. She does nothing. The bandits and gobbers run amok in our land, the peasants organize and protest."

"Perhaps I could talk with her?"

Harvald smiled. For a moment he slipped out of his royal plurality. "I think that could be arranged. I think perhaps you could even help her."

"I'd be happy to try. What do you have in mind?"

That conniving look was back now that Andrillia was gone. "Vengeance satisfied can be a great motivator. You see, our inconsolable dragon's mate was killed quite brutally some time back. His name was —"

Realization came home. "Fang the Dread."

He smiled. "Fang the Dread."

"What about the girl?"

"She'll be our guest. We'll tell her that we escorted you to the border and sent you on your way. Of course, you'll be dead by then. A bony, gristly meal I have no doubt."

Despite my sudden discomfort, I was impressed. "You've gotten quite good at this, Harvald. You wear the crown the well."

"Thank you." He shifted its weight on his head and scratched his scalp. "It itches."

$\mathcal{Y}$ou never forget your first dragon. I met mine on the day I asked Luendyl to be my wife.

Giants are one thing, all blunder and bulk, but dragons are lean, mean, liquid grace.

Fang the Dread was no exception. The first time I saw him, he was outlined against a full moon, hovering and preparing to dive on an unsuspecting village. I sat on a hillside, studying him while Luendyl slept. I prodded her.

"He's here, darling."

She stirred and sat up, the blankets spilling around her and the moonlight glinting off her armor. On work nights, she often slept ready for the fight.

Fang dove, disappearing behind a barn, then lifted with a bellowing cow clutched tightly in his talons. The dragon turned east. Below, lights came on and shouts were raised.

Luendyl wadded her blankets into a tight ball and shoved them into her saddlebags. "Let's go then."

I leaped onto Falgron's back, mentally checking off the list we'd created two nights before. "Follow him home. Take his head. Take his treasure. Collect our reward."

"Exactly." She surged forward. Her steed, Frazen, was considerably faster than Falgron. I pressed to keep up.

We tore across the fields and through copses of alder and beech, leaping streams and skirting ponds. We followed that damnable dragon for six hours. The sun rose on our pursuit, the sky moving from gray to mauve. The pounding hooves and flapping wings drowned out any birdsong.

Then he vanished behind a mounded hill.

I reined in. Luendyl, just a bit ahead of me now, did the same. "Do you think this is it?"

I shook my head. "I think he saw us."

She laughed. "That's impossible. He hasn't looked back once."

"Maybe he heard us. Or smelled us."

She sauntered towards me. "Andro, I think it's highly un —"

Did I mention lean, mean, liquid grace? Three things happened at once. Fang dropped like a heavy stone from nowhere. A large, bloody cow plowed into me and tumbled me to the ground. Luendyl lifted off her horse and into the air to race east in the clutches of Fang the Dread.

One word, bellowed gleefully as Fang hurled his dinner at me, reverberated in the morning air. "Virgin!"

I climbed back onto Falgron and spurred us after her. She had managed to draw one of her scimitars and hacked at Fang's ankle, raising sparks. Fang accelerated and increased altitude. I'm not sure if any words passed between them, but Luendyl suddenly stopped hacking and settled in for the ride. She'd always loved flying. Fang leveled out, descended a bit, and sped on. I tried to tell myself that she was screaming in terror. That's what she's always maintained. And though she denied it to the very end, I still think she was actually *laughing*. Giggling like a little girl.

"Hang on, love," I yelled after her. I doubt she heard. But I needed to say it more than she needed to hear it. I pushed Falrgon harder that day than any day before. We stayed a nudge behind the dragon's shadow as it coursed over the meadows and hills. Eventually, we hit the wall of an enormous cliff. Above, Fang scuttled three-legged over a ledge, careful not to bang or squeeze his newfound prize overmuch, and disappeared into the mountainside.

I dismounted. I stood at the base of the cliff and stared up, scratching my head beneath my helmet. Personally, I thought Oingeltonken was a dangerous wizard and the only good that had ever come from his enchantments was my wife crashing down into my life years before. But in that moment, for the first time, I actually wished for a pair of those Flights of Fancy Winged Shoes. But in the end, I had to do it the old-fashioned way. I dug the rope and grapnel hook out of the bottom of my saddlebags, turned Falgron loose to graze, and started climbing.

Halfway up, dented and dusty, I paused to rest and re-set my hook. Sounds drifted down. Deep, rumbling noises from the cave entrance above.

The dragon, it seemed, was singing.

Love songs.

To my girl.

I climbed faster.

"Fair and buxom maiden show to me your wares," I heard Fang sing as I pulled myself onto the ledge. The large cave stretched back into the mountain, as dark and menacing as the beast's mouth. Piles of meat-laced bone lined the entrance. Remnants of cows, horses, villagers. The stink overwhelmed my nose and sent tears into my beard and down the neck of my chain mail shirt. I stretched out on the rock, catching my breath.

The deep bass voice paused, then shifted to cooing. "Such a sparkly, shiny virgin."

I crawled to my knees and drew my sword. I stood.

"Fang the Dread!"

The cooing stopped. Deep in the cave, I heard the rustle of scales on metal. Sword leveled, I entered the reeking lair. Odors shifted the further I walked. A touch of vanilla mixed with the rotting meat. Dim light flickered ahead. A voice bellowed out. "Who calls my name?"

I should've kept quiet. But I rarely do. "Your so-called virgin's man."

Fang lowered his voice. "You didn't say you were married."

Luendyl answered; I could tell she was amused. "Oh, we're not married." She raised her voice for my benefit I suppose. "Not yet anyway."

By now, I'd turned a corner and could see. The massive cavern lay in the guttering shadows of a dozen large scented candles. Fang the Dread crouched in a pile of treasure, Luendyl clutched loosely in a claw. His head weaved back and forth, one emerald eye watching her and the other watching the entrance.

I sucked in my breath. He made the giants look small and insignificant. Still, I strode into the candlelight and raised my sword. Fang watched me but kept talking to her.

"But you *are* a virgin?"

Luendyl shrugged. "Well. Not exactly."

Fang howled in agony. "Not exactly?"

I stepped closer. I couldn't help but grin as I thought about *how* 'not exactly' she was. "Not by a long shot," I said.

"Andro," she said, "You're not helping."

Fang's eyes narrowed. "What does *not exactly* mean . . . exactly?"

I think I saw her blush a bit in the candlelight. I watched her lips move as she silently counted off names on her fingers. Naturally, I knew we weren't one another's first. But I think every man wants to believe he's no more than second. Or maybe third. I made myself look away as she finished her first hand and started on the other.

"Um . . . what are we counting?"

Fang howled again. I suddenly wanted to join him.

Fang tightened his grip on her. "You are either a virgin," he said, "Or you are lunch. Which is it?"

"Oh. Definitely a virgin."

I'd gotten close enough that coins were clinking beneath my feet. Fang's head moved quickly until it was just a few feet from me. His eyes dilated. His huge mouth opened, easily the size of a small door. "And what say *you*? Do you concur?"

"I guess that depends," I said.

"Upon what?"

"What happens if she *is* a virgin?"

I had never seen a dragon shrug before. It is a terrible thing. Bits of gold flew up, the room shook. "I still eat her. Just more slowly. By candlelight." I had also never seen a dragon grin before. It's equally terrible. "With a bit of soft music and a vat or two of wine."

I moved to the left just in time. His snout came down, jaws snapping where I had stood. I didn't know what else to do, so I shoved my sword into his ear.

Fang roared and twisted, snapping off my blade at the hilt. He let Luendyl go and dug at the sword in his ear with a long talon. She scrambled to my side, drawing her scimitar. "Took you long enough," she said.

I tossed the hilt aside and looked around the treasure mound. I spotted a large axe and waded through the gold towards it. Fang thrashed, shaking the room, and I fell into the gold. Luendyl leapt aside, bringing her blade down on the dragon's neck. The enchanted steel sparked on his scales. "I don't think this is working," she said.

I grabbed up the axe and rolled as his mouth again fell. I heard a crunch as his fangs struck the hard stone floor. When his head came up again, blood and gold spilled from his mouth. I swung the axe up, driving it diagonally into his gums at the base of one massive tooth. Luendyl put her scimitar into his other ear, and though her blade held together, it was yanked from her hand as he jerked away.

Suddenly, the vanilla scent lost itself in the smell of hot sulphur. Smoke billowed from his nostrils as Fang snapped his mouth shut. "He's going to flame!" I shouted at Luendyl.

She moved. His tail whipped around and sent her into the air to land heavily on the other side of the cavern. She didn't move.

We'd fought dozens of battles together. We'd killed hundreds of foes. We'd faced danger and death at every turn for most of our three years together. For the first time, I realized I could lose her. Could have already lost her. Something broke inside me and my own roaring matched the sound of the flames blasting from the dragon's mouth. I raced towards her, a trail of fire chasing my heels.

"Luendyl?" I scooped her up and kept running. "Not this way," I said to no one in particular. "Not this way." Fire singed the hair on the back of my neck.

We left the cave and I laid her out on the ledge behind an outcropping of rock. Her eyes fluttered.

"Not what way?" she asked.

That was the first and last time she ever saw me cry. "We're supposed to grow old together," I told her.

The cavern was quiet behind us. I looked back over my shoulder.

"Well?" she asked.

"Wait here."

Dragons, ever the arrogant lot, never suspect that those who live to run away might return willingly . . . or in a calculated rage. Fang lay growling on his back, claws digging at the blades in his ears, long tongue licking at his wounded gums. He did not hear me. But he did smell me. He craned his neck and squinted into the smoke that still hung in the air.

"You're *back?*"

I said nothing. I hefted the axe and planted it in his open mouth. With my bare hands, I pried free the tooth I had loosened. He yowled, his claws rasping against the metal of my armor. I felt hot fire where they tore through and ripped my skin.

"We're supposed to grow old together," I told the dragon as I shoved his own fang deep into his throat. It pushed easily through the scales, and with a final roar, Fang the Dread jerked, heaved, and then lay still.

"We will, Andro," Luendyl said from behind me. I didn't realize she had followed me back into the lair. I turned towards her, my hands shaking, the giant tooth slippery with both my blood and Fang's.

"Promise?" I asked.

"Promise," she said.

I fell into her arms and she held me up. Looking back, I can see that she's always held me up.

She was frying dragon steaks on a small fire when I regained consciousness. I was bandaged and feeling better — it ends up that dragons keep well-stocked medicine chests.

Luendyl poured five hundred-year-old wine into diamond goblets and served up dinner on ruby-encrusted platinum platters. "I'm going to want a ring," she said.

I looked at the treasure mound. "I'm sure we can find something."

"And a *real* wedding. Handen Hall should do nicely."

"Whatever you want, love."

She looked at me carefully. The light softened her face, and for a moment she didn't look fierce at all, only fair. Absolutely the fairest. "Are you sure about this, Andro?"

"We're supposed to grow old together," I said again.

She nodded, sipped her wine, then pointed her fork at my plate. "How's your steak?"

"It's good," I said. "Tastes like chicken."

reya the Dark's lair was nothing like her husband's all those years ago.

It was more a mud hole than a cave, set deep in the mountains on Grunland's northern border. The guards had hauled me there by wagon and deposited me, un-shackled, at the mouth of a hole carved into the muddy clay. They gave me my pack and my wife and stood waiting, swords drawn, for me to go inside.

"Thanks, boys," I said.

They kept waiting.

"I can take it from here."

They said nothing.

Finally, I turned my back on them and entered the hole. Dirty sunlight followed me in, casting a gray gloom over the lair. "Hello?"

I heard something large stir. "Are you the surprise they told me about?"

"Maybe," I said.

"The one that's supposed to cheer me up?"

"Quite possibly, yes."

Again, the stirring. "Come closer then. I can barely see you."

I moved into the larger room. Breya coughed flame

and a torch guttered to life. The room was sparse. The dragon lay along the wall in a trough roughly the size of her body.

"And who exactly are you? Another acrobat?"

"No," I said.

"A juggler?"

"No."

"Magician?"

I shook my head. "No."

"Good. Can't abide any of them. Ran the last one off with his robes ablaze." Her eyes moved over me. "Then what are you?"

I thought about lying but suddenly I felt tired of it all. No point lying to her or to myself. I'd come to the end of it and I would die on my feet. "My name is Andro Giantslayer. I killed your husband."

Her head came up fast. "My husband?"

I swallowed and closed my eyes, waiting for the fire or the teeth. Nothing happened.

"And they sent you up here thinking that would make me feel better?"

I opened my eyes. "Yes. I think Harvald said something about me being a gristly, bony meal."

Breya laughed. "Not even a meal. More like a snack. Still, there's one flaw in this plan of his."

"What's that?"

"My husband wasn't killed. He just got sick and died. Some giants we used to play Pillage and Plunder with buried him out in Alderland."

"Same as my Luendyl," I said. That hollow, empty space was back in my stomach.

"Your what?"

I sat down, cradling my wife on my lap. "My Luendyl," I said. "She just got sick and died."

Uncomfortable silence settled between us. "Well," she said, "What do we do now?"

I shrugged. "They're waiting out there for you to eat me or burn me or something."

"For killing my husband?"

I chuckled. "I didn't *think* Fang was marriage material. Not the way he went after the virgins."

"Tell me about it. Fang was . . ." She paused. "Wait a minute. You killed *Fang*?"

"Yes. Fang the Dread. Did you know him?"

"Now it makes more sense." Her head moved towards me, her glittering claws tearing into the mud. "Fang was my *first* husband."

I clutched my urn and waited. Again, nothing happened.

"Thought your wife was a virgin, I'll wager," she finally said. "Candles. Music. I know all about it. Certainly wasn't the first time. That's why I left the bastard."

I nodded. "We weren't married yet. But still . . ."

"But still," she said. "I remember feeling glad that someone finally put him out of my misery. Disgusting worm."

Silence settled in again. I leaned against the muddy wall, tracing the outline of the urn. Breya watched me. I've always disliked uncomfortable, quiet patches along the way but time and time again, my interruptions of those silences have taken me down difficult roads.

"The first year or two are the hardest," she finally said.

I looked up at her. "Does it get better after that?"

"No. Not really. You just get used to it."

"Oh."

"I suppose there are things you can do, though, to make it a bit more bearable." She snorted. "Not that I've had much use for that."

"Like what?" I asked.

"Oh, talking about it. Staying busy. And there are books out there, too."

"Well, I've stayed pretty busy." I dug around in my pack, pulled out Clovis's copy of *Venison Stew for the Heart* and held it up. "I'm not much of a reader, but a friend gave me this."

Outside, a horse neighed. Low voices conversed.

"Blast and bother," Breya said. "Are *they* still waiting?"

"I suspect so."

She stretched out, her neck twisting and extending down the passage. "Yes. Still waiting. We'll have to do something about that."

I put the book away, picked the urn back up. Strange to have so much of my life reduced to ashes and memories. During the long walk to Grunland, the conversations with Andrillia and the others, it had been easier not to think about it. "What do you have in mind?"

She snapped her tongue over her lips. "I think you should scream really, really loud."

I screamed. Breya thrashed her tail, sending mud and water down the passage. I kept screaming until she nodded for me to stop.

"There," she bellowed to the guards outside. "He's finished. You can go home now."

A few minutes later, I heard the wagon clatter away.

"So what now?" she asked.

I set the urn down. "We could talk, I suppose."

"Do you want to talk?"

"Not really. Do you?"

"No. Not really." She lowered her head back into the mud. "What about that book?"

"Fey and halflet bare-the-soul and talk-about-our-feelings crap," I said. "Anyone carting around a five-year-old in their head needs a walloping if you ask me."

She laughed. "Still, it might pass the time."

I pulled the book out. "Might be good for a chuckle or two, I suppose."

So I flipped it open, found a story and started to read.

The first one was about Pyflee the One-Winged Pixie who, despite her obvious deformity, still managed to win the Gildis Fairy Air Marathon pennant three times running.

"Ridiculous," Breya snorted.

"Preposterous," I added.

Then I read about Orgle the Obese, a troll with an uncontrollable appetite for pickled dwarf feet who, after falling in love with a dwarven princess, became a vegetarian, lost three hundred pounds, and founded a crutch factory.

"Who writes these?" Breya asked.

"No idea," I said. "But the crutch bit is clever."

Next, I read about a king who hated music and a minstrel who hated kings and how, after being stranded together in the belly of a lactose intolerant giant, they gained an appreciation of one another's jobs by trading places for a year. The king won Shaluzan's contest and the minstrel won three major wars and annexed half another kingdom.

"Well, that's at least plausible," I said.

"Barely," Breya said.

Last, I read about Gilda the Troll Wife, whose husband died in some silly, senseless way, and how she spent the first dozen years doing absolutely nothing and the second dozen years doing absolutely anything just to keep her mind off the big hole in her heart and —

I closed the book. "I think that's enough of that."

She sighed. "I think so, too. Silly, pointless book."

I tucked the book back into my pack. It was my turn to ask. "What now?"

She shrugged. "We should do something."

"Want to get out for bit?" I asked.

She stretched her wings and cracked her neck. "What do you have in mind?"

"I have an idea. Do you like minstrels?"

She shuddered. "They make me gassy."

"You'll like this one. She's a good kid. We'll just need to rescue her first."

She thought about it for a moment. "I've never actually been on the other end of the rescuing bit. Might be nice for a change."

I gathered up my wife and my pack. I climbed onto Breya's back. "Go easy on me," I said. "I've never flown dragon before."

She bucked forward, snaking for the entrance. "Well, you know what they say?"

Outside the cave, she unfurled the fullness of her wings and beat against the air. "No," I answered. "What do they say?"

She plunged upward, gravity pushing me down into her scales. "Once you go dragon, you wish for a wagon!"

I groaned. "We should send that one in. It belongs in the book somewhere."

"Hang on," she said. And I did.

And suddenly, I understood why Luendyl laughed so long ago and why she always said that I should give her back to the sky.

This is the part I don't want to write. If you don't want to read it, skip on ahead. I'll meet you down the road.

Luendyl the Fierce and Fair, Fiercest and Fairest, went to sleep on Godsfeast Eve and never woke up.

She'd been sick. Coughing. Sore. Fevered. But she'd been all these things before. We'd decided that if she were no better the next morning, I would make the trip to town and see what the apothecary had for remedies. I made her some soup and sat with her while she ate it in bed.

"Still no word from Karysa?" she asked.

I shook my head. "She and the League went north. That Witch Queen in Nebios is acting up again."

She nodded, slurping at the soup. "Glad she got the League back together. I wonder what Ansabel is up to?"

Ansabel was our daughter's partner. Daughter of some duke or count that she had rescued from certain doom. They made their home near Handen Hall and talked a lot about adopting, though I suppose they could've charmed Azerminus into a revision of his Egg Charming Elixir.

I shrugged. "I'm not sure. She's probably with her parents for the feast."

She finished her dinner and I took the bowl away. I put it in the sink and went back to her. Coughing, she patted the quilt beside her. "Come back to bed, Andro."

I stretched out next to her and held her hand. "You'll feel better tomorrow, love. If not, I'll go see what Bremble has on his shelves."

"I might not, Andro."

"You will," I said.

"But if I didn't . . ."

I shushed her. Something she hated, but she didn't say anything this time. She drew in a deep breath. I heard the rattling in her lungs.

She was always good at figuring out how to say her piece. I think maybe that's one of the keys to a good marriage — knowing how to talk to the other person about something they don't want to talk about. "You haven't been fishing in a while," she said.

"No. Busy with other things."

"You can never be too busy for what you love," she said. "I want you to remember that."

I laughed. "Remember. Hell, woman, it's what you've taught me from the start. That night in the Blastlands? Danger lurking all about and me rutting like a schoolboy with a goddess who'd fallen from the sky?"

She chuckled. "That was a good time."

"They've all been good times."

"Or that time on the Grunland throne? And on Fang's treasure pile?"

I twisted and looked at her, squeezing her hand. "Not just those times. All of our times. Everything good and perfect in my life came from you."

"And Karysa," she added.

"Must I remind you where *she* came from?"

She snorted a bit. "No need. I remember that well enough."

"I rest my case."

She let go of my hand, then stroked it lightly with her fingers. "I need to rest mine, too," she said.

I kissed her cheek. "Get some sleep, love. I'll see you in the morning."

She smiled at me. Then she said the same thing she always said, whether I was staying up late, heading to town, or gallivanting off to do a hero's work. "Don't be too long. I'll miss you too much."

And I said what I always say: "Be back before you know I'm gone."

She went to sleep. She didn't wake up the next morning. Or the next. Or the next. On that third day, I shed no tears when I put the torch to my wife.

Ashes and memories.

*N*o doubt, you've heard about the Rescue of Andrillia Songweaver from one of her own songs. Her exceptionally deft usage of poetic license is commendable.

It actually went something like this.

Breya and I crashed through the glass dome of Harvald's throne room, showering the room with a rainbow of glittering shards.

The guards scattered. Harvald jumped up, his behind catching in the throne and carrying it up with him. He toppled and fell over. Breya landed heavily in the center of the room.

"Where's the girl?" I asked.

Harvald lay on the floor, whimpering. I looked around. One of his chancellors cowered nearby, mouth hanging open. I pointed. "You. She's here in two minutes or my friend starts roasting."

The chancellor tore out of the room. I remember wondering if he really would find Andrillia or just keep running. It didn't matter. Andrillia arrived two minutes later. I pulled her up behind me and we were airborne again.

She grinned. "I knew you'd come back for me."

"Andrillia . . . Breya. Breya . . . Andrillia, the minstrel I was telling you about."

Andrillia clutched at my shirt. "This is *definitely* going into the song."

"You may need to dress it up a bit."

"Oh, I will. Don't worry."

We hit Breya's optimal cruising altitude. She whipped her head around to look at us. "Where to now?"

"The Blastlands," Andrillia said. "A short flight?"

I nodded. "Is that okay?"

"Yes," they both said. And we were off.

*J*ust another push," the midwife said.

"I'm tired of pushing," Luedyl said through gritted teeth. "Get that baby out of me or I'll carve you in half."

Always helpful, I squeezed her hand. "We sold off the scimitars, love."

"Andro, you're not help —" The words were lost as her growl became a shout. Sweat poured down her face. I used my other hand to run the damp cloth over her forehead.

I looked at the hand she held. In her grip, the tips of my fingers were as white as her knuckles. "Sorry, darling."

"Just push," the midwife said again. "It'll be over before you know it."

"Then let's trade places, you gibber sucking rat licker." She roared again. I thought I heard bones crunching in my hand.

Azerminus poked his head into the room. "Is everything going —" His face went white. "Oh my. Excuse me." He disappeared.

I can't remember exactly what Luendyl said next, something about where she was going to put the next Egg Charming Elixir he concocted. It evoked a painful image.

Then a new voice entered the room. A high, warbling cry that I couldn't ever imagine growing to love as much as I did.

After, with the baby cleaned up and wrapped in a blanket, I sat with Luendyl and our daughter.

Tears ran down my wife's face. "Oh, look at her, Andro. She has your nose."

It was a lot smaller, but I could see it. I didn't know what to say. "She has your ears."

"No she doesn't. Those are yours too."

I laughed. "She's doomed then."

"Not if she has her mother's sensibilities."

"True. What do we call her?"

We'd never been able to decide. We'd tossed out

Andro and Andrillia straight away. Dozens of other names
I can't remember were also pitched and tossed over
the months as we built our home and settled in to
Brookwood Down.

Luendyl looked up at me. "What was the name of
that princess?"

"Which one?"

"The one we went to rescue? The one that Duke
What's-It hired those ogres to kidnap so he could force
her hand in marriage?"

"Oh. *Her?*"

"Yes. *Her.*" The baby made strange gurgling sounds.
"Why her?"

She shifted her bundle, baring her breast. "Remember? We got there and —"

I laughed. "And she'd somehow managed to take
on the whole lot by herself. Asked us to take her
straightway to Duke Grandor's hunting palace so she
could take him on as well."

"Exactly. Left quite a mess of him, too."

I scratched my head. "I don't remember her name.
Karyla? Karyna?"

"Karysa," Luendyl said.

"Karysa?"

She nodded. "That was a girl who could take care
of herself."

I leaned in and kissed her. "So are you. Maybe we should call her Luendyl the Fierce."

"And Fair," she said. "You always leave that bit out."

"Sorry."

"It's okay." She rubbed the baby's chin with the tip of her finger. "Karysa. What do you think of that?"

"Ogres beware," I said.

"And dukes," my wife added, smiling down on the life we had made together. "Don't forget dukes."

*W*e entered the Blastlands before dawn. The night had slipped past, Breya and Andrillia making small talk about songs and dragons and treasure while I kept quiet and thought about everything that had brought me to this place.

"You're terribly quiet," Andrillia said.

"Just thinking," I answered. The sky around us took on the color of steel. I was watching as the ground below grayed as well, scanning the horizon for the desolate ruins that had become the birthplace of life and love for me so many years ago. "Might turn a bit south," I said to Breya.

"Ghul-Shar-Tov, right?"

"Yes."

"It's not far." She banked a bit. Steel became deep purple and then pink. I looked over my shoulder to see the sun crest the Dragon's Spine Mountains. That's when I saw her, racing across the sky to meet us.

Luendyl, glittering in her armor, legs moving tirelessly to the beat of Oingeltonken's Flights of Fancy Winged Shoes. I opened my mouth and would have pointed if I didn't need to hang on.

Andrillia turned to look. "What is it?" But she

couldn't see. Maybe the angle was wrong.

She moved across heaven, my Luendyl, her arms stretching out and her mouth opening. My tears made her glitter all the more. She drew closer and I heard her call out.

"Dad!"

Not Luendyl. Karysa. A spark, a puff of smoke, and the left shoe cut out. Oingeltonken's left shoes were ever his bane. She spun, trying to regain control, but at this altitude there would be no slowing the fall. And no tent below to catch her. She plummeted, hands still stretched out.

Now Andrillia saw her. "Is that — ?"

"Breya," I shouted, "Can you catch her?"

The dragon said nothing. She just spun and dove; we hung on as best we could. Air rushed past. I could see my daughter flailing below, digging frantically in her pouch for some bit of scroll or potion. Breya's mouth reached her before the rest of us. She caught Karysa in her jaws.

Andrillia and I cheered. "Well done," I said.

Breya made some muffled response.

"Don't talk with your mouth full," my daughter said.

We landed on the floor of the Blastlands. I slid down from Breya's back and hugged Karysa.

"Dad, what are you doing out here without me?"

She looked tired. Her eyes were red and puffy. "Why didn't you wait?"

I felt my shoulders sag. "I sent the birds out. No one came."

"We were up north. Remember? Nebios?"

I actually had forgotten. Or not made the connections. Now I know it was just the grief. It clouds you. It fogs you in. But in that moment I remembered. "The Witch Queen? How did that go?"

Karysa looked angry and sad at the same time. "We'll finish up with her later. As soon as we got the message, we turned south."

"We?"

A large patch of carpet settled onto ground beside us. A wizened old man stepped off, followed by a grizzled warrior and a grouchy dwarf lord.

Azerminus walked quickly over and put his arms around me. "Old friend," he said, "I'm so sorry for your loss." Fenruk's large hand came down on my shoulder. Dunder stood apart, looking somber. Azerminus stepped back.

"We came as soon as we could," Fenruk said, joining the wizard.

"We had to fight our way back," Karysa The White of the West said. "Where's Mom?"

I pulled the urn from my pack. "She's here."

No one spoke for a bit. Finally, I said the right thing. "Karysa, I'm sorry. I should have waited longer."

She softened a bit. "You should have. But we all knew it could happen someday. And you really had no way of knowing when . . . or even *if* I could get back." She hugged me again. "At least we found you."

"Was I hard to find?"

"Not too hard," she said. "You left a pretty wide trail. That last bit with the King's Throne Room in Grunland . . . that was priceless." She looked up. I followed her gaze and saw the ruins on the horizon. "But I knew eventually you'd end up out here."

Azerminus conjured chairs for us. Breya stretched out in the sun. Andrillia sat wide-eyed and listened until someone called on her for a song. She sang. We ate and drank and told stories about Luendyl the Fierce and Fair.

When the moon rose over the Blastlands, Karysa and I climbed onto Breya's back. The lost city of Ghul-Shar-Tov shone silver below us as she lifted us into the air. She began to fly in a widening circle, wings stretched out in the moonlight. Laughing and crying at the same time, Karysa and I opened the urn and gave her mother — my wife — back to the sky.

*S*pring is coming on now. New life is showing in the leaves. Brookwood Down is quiet these days, but for the birds and creek and the occasional song.

Karysa and Ansabel informally adopted Andrillia. I guess that makes me informally a grandfather. They've come to visit a time or two. She always brings her lute and plays our song. Alas, Andrillia did not win the Emperor's contest. But somehow, she did manage to win the heart of one of his thirty-seven sons. I'm hoping it's a long courtship, but her new parents will help with that.

The Broadback boys added on to my barn and now Breya comes and goes as she pleases. She's started dating . . . something I doubt I'll do . . . and she even went a few rounds with a certain perfumed centaur acquaintance of mine. How they managed, I dare not ask. Azerminus has been out at least a half dozen times and swears he's hauling me up to Handen Hall for some kind of lifetime achievement medal they're tossing about these days. I'll most likely go. And I'll smile a lot and think about my wife and the times we shared both there and everywhere else.

So why have I filled these pages up? I look at them, quite a stack, though I'll wager nothing like Orvid and Drimbull's *Venison Stew for the Heart*. What's it all about, really?

I think if I've learned anything, in the very end, it's this. The grandest adventures of our lives aren't about horses and swords and ghost cities lost to time. They are the choices we've made and why we've made them. And the greatest treasures in our lives aren't the sleeping vaults beneath moon-misted ruins or the treasure mounds of flaming dragons. They are the people we have loved and been loved by along the path of our choices. And the most sweeping battles we will ever fight are not against gibbers, gobbers, giants, or trolls. They are against other foes — any foes that stand between us and our true treasures in the adventure of our living.

I've heard many good words along the way. You'll remember these, I'm sure:

Often the things we love best are what we expect least. Your companions will ever be your saving grace. You can never be too busy for what you love.

And now my tale is done. By my own measure, I've had a great adventure full of unexpected wealth along the way.

Now those damnable trout are calling my name. Oingeltonken has supposedly perfected a self-casting rod. I'm going to try it out with some trepidation and some worms I dug out of the garden last night.

I've set the skillet out. I'm planning fish for dinner.

A Meandering Afterword
Complete with Acknowledgements

*I*n November 2004, I sat down at my keyboard and typed: "I shed no tears when I put the torch to my wife." After that, I sat back and said "Hmmm." At the time, I wasn't really sure where I was going or what would be waiting at the end. Some of my stories get outlined carefully over time with me waiting patiently (or not) for the story to cook before I actually start writing. Some of them are just a first line and a vague notion and me flying by the seat of my pants.

Last Flight of the Goddess was that last kind. For nearly two months, I typed away at this little story about a retired hero named Andro Giantslayer, his wife Luendyl the Fierce and Fair, and their lives in a quirky fantasy setting peppered with twenty-first century sensibilities. (Really, folks, wouldn't magic be useful for birth control and diapers? And which way DO centaurs swing?) Each scene unfolded seemingly without much thought or effort. I've heard tell of stories that "just seemed to write themselves" or characters who "came to life and told me what to say." This was the first time I ever felt that pull.

I wrote it scene by scene, reading it aloud to my wife wherever she happened to be at the time I finished. Tub, kitchen, bed — it didn't matter. And if I went more than a few days, she'd ask "When are you going to write the next scene about Andro and Luendyl?" And I'd grumble and make excuses, but in the end, I went back to it because . . . well, I wanted to know what happened next, too.

In many ways, it's about Jen and me, though you can ask anyone: I am no hero. But she *is* a goddess.

It's also about journeys, about treasure, and about the intersections we cross in our lives.

Take the intersection I crossed around Christmas of 1980 (or thereabouts.)

My best friend — Bobby then, now Robert — called me up to tell me that he'd gotten this amazing new game. The next time I was over, he broke it out and I was immediately suspicious.

First of all, there wasn't even a board (though there was a map that he got to look at but I did not.) Nor were there any pieces (though this was quickly remedied by a plethora of tiny little lead figures that we meticulously painted when we weren't busy playing.)

There was a book. And another book. And a lot of dice. Holy Cow, were there ever dice! Dice like I had never seen before, with four sides and six sides and eight sides and ten sides and twenty sides, in bright colors. "And," Bobby told me, "we don't need a board because we play the game with our brains."

And gosh-wow, did we ever play! I'll never forget that first game. After an hour or two of creating my character (including a carefully drawn illustration by yours truly) good old Akroden strode boldly into the dungeon and was forthwith slain by animated skeletons in the first room he entered.

"Wasn't THAT fun," Bobby said with evil glee.

"No, not really," I replied, wiping my nose on my sleeve and trying not to cry.

But we got better at it. We took turns, we introduced more of our friends (Chris, Dave, Jason, Joel, the other Dave, and others), tried to teach our younger siblings, and it became a way of life through most of middle and high school. Along the way, we created elaborate maps and campaigns and . . . you guessed it: *stories*. Elaborate stories full of twists and turns, romance and betrayal. Stories full of *characters* — both protagonists and antagonists, leading roles and supporting cast. And our characters developed and changed, wrestled with problems, and either emerged victorious and wealthy or (in the case of my elvish warrior-burglar) maimed but happy to be alive.

Though I don't play it anymore, I still say that little game changed my life. Apart from the amazing storytelling mechanism — the give and take of the reader/writer relationship, the bliss of being "immersed in story" — I also learned rudimentary budgeting, advanced relationship management, problem-solving, map-making, and, to a degree, strategic planning. All from a game without a board, a game that we played with our brains.

Of course, lots of people screamed about it. The corruption of young minds, the physical manifestation of Satan Lucifer his own bad self — you know, that same thing folks started screaming about the adventures of a certain boy wizard not so very long ago.

That was an important intersection that eventually led to this little book.

Here's another:

In 1997, I came back to writing after more than ten years away from it. In that intersection, I attended my first critique workshop and met another great friend, John Pitts — my very first writing pal. (Ask him sometime about the *Venison Stew for the Heart* references.) He's had a watchful eye on everything I've written since the day we became friends, and that eye has made all the difference again and again.

While in that same intersection, I started submitting stories to a local magazine called *Talebones*. In 1998, I met the Amazing Swensons when I accepted their invitation to attend a writing class they were teaching. These amazing folks not only taught one helluva of a writing class (where we actually wrote and critiqued one another's work on a weekly basis), but they also took me under their wing, introducing me to the wide, wide world of cons and con-folk. And in 2000, they published my first story. And in 2001 they published another.

That 2001 sale took me into yet another intersection: that fashionably savvy reincarnation of the Polynesian Sportswear God known as Jay Lake. He said nice things about that little story about a walking bear in a review he wrote for *Tangent Online* and it led to a pretty amazing friendship with a pretty amazing Force of Literary Nature who's taught me a lot about both the business and the practice of writing . . . in addition to being an all-around great guy. Now he's saying nice things about me and my work again in the front of this slender little volume — I'm very grateful and couldn't think of a better person for the job. And those Amazing Swensons, after putting some of my first stories into print, are now putting out my first stand-alone project. And I couldn't think of better folks for *that* job either.

Having Patrick and Honna and Jay involved in this venture just feels . . . well . . . *poetic*, I reckon.

And one more intersection:

In 2002, a fiery redhead landed in my camp and I had no idea at the time that she was a goddess. I was camped out in the Blastlands — well, okay, it was Longview, Washington — and in many ways I'd just hit reset on my own adventure. She showed up when I least expected and she exceeded my wildest imaginings of joy. She has been an amazing companion with me on the journey so far, and this story is first and foremost for her. She really is the fiercest and the fairest of them all, with or without the scimitars.

All of these words are simply to acknowledge the great debt I owe all of these people who've intersected with me along the way. They all brought treasure into my life, making me the richest man I know. Oh, there are more that I could list. But you get my drift: Gratitude is the watch-word.

I could have probably said it better and shorter. Maybe Andro Giantslayer said it best of all:

My companions will ever be my saving grace.

Ken Scholes
Gresham, Oregon
August 2006

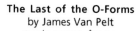

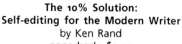
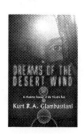

About the Author

Ken Scholes is a Pacific Northwest original, growing up in a small logging town Southeast of Seattle at the foot of Mt. Rainier. Ken started crafting stories at a young age and started submitting for publication in high school.

Years later, he sold his first story to *Talebones* after attending a writing class taught by editors Patrick and Honna Swenson. Since then, he's sold short fiction to *Weird Tales, Realms of Fantasy, Aeon, Fortean Bureau, Shimmer* and *Son & Foe*. He also has work appearing in the anthologies *Polyphony 6, TEL:Stories, Best of the Rest 3, Best of the Rest 4*, and *L. Ron Hubbard Presents Writers of the Future Volume XXI*.

Ken lives in Gresham, Oregon, with the utterly divine Jen West Scholes. By day, he works as a civil servant, processing government contracts and procurements.

Ken can be found and contacted through his website at www.sff.net/people/kenscholes.

Printed in the United States
135727LV00001B/1/A